This book
belongs to

_____

_____

The House on Haunted Hill

Written by **Slade Stone**

Illustrated by **John Jordan and Leigh Anna Thompson**

It was a cold, eerie night in Booville. The wind howled through the bare trees. The branches clawed at the sky. Owls screeched. Bats shrieked.

A full moon rose. From out of the night there came high-pitched squeals and screams…

"Oh, stop it! You're scaring me!" said Wilson.

"M-m-my knees are sh-shaking!" said Kate.

"But it's all true!" said Francine. "I was there. That's just how it was… up on Haunted Hill! Those strange squealy sounds came from right out of that—*that house!*"

"But no one has lived there for years," whispered Wilson.

"For 152 years, to be exact," added Frank Junior.
"Well, someone lives there now! I saw candles in the windows.
I saw smoke coming from the chimneys. And that squeal—"
Francine shivered. "It was real, all right! Someone should go
and find out what's up there!"

"You can't mean one of us…" said Kate meekly.

"Count me out!" cried Denton, pulling his cape around himself.

"No way!" said Wilson, nervously fiddling with his wrapping.

"This does not sound like a venture to which I could commit myself," said Frank Junior, who was turning greener.

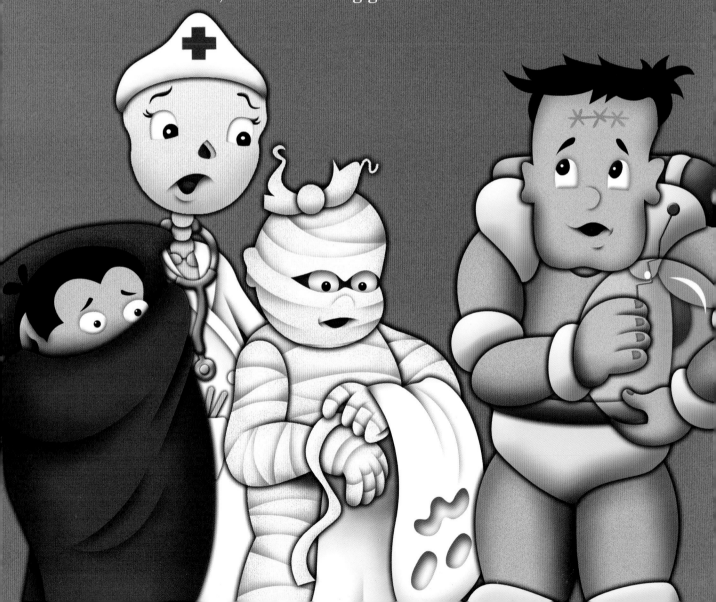

"What a bunch of scaredy cats!" exclaimed Francine. "And you—" (pointing a finger at Frank Junior) "—my very own brother—afraid of an old house! Well, I'm going up there tonight after Halloweening. This is the best mystery to hit Booville in a long time, and I want to find out what's in that house. So…" (smoothing her hair) "…which one of you is going with me?"

"Not me!" squeaked Kate.
"Not me!" chimed in Denton.
"Not I!" said Frank Junior.
Everyone turned to stare at Frank Junior.
"Not… I?" asked Denton with a sneer.
"It's grammatically correct," said Frank Junior. "You see, the subject of the—"

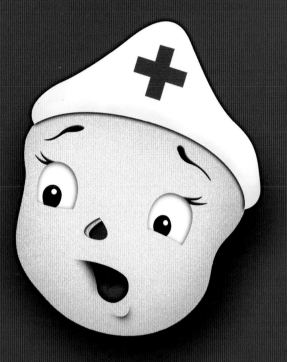
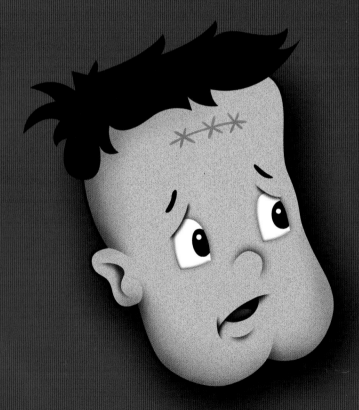

"All right, we believe you. You *are* the smartest kid in Booville," broke in Francine. She turned to Wilson, who was still fidgeting. "Wilson?"

"Er... ah... not me. I mean I. I mean *not* I."

Francine leaned forward and glared at Wilson.

Wilson swallowed. He knew he was doomed.

That night, the plan was set. The Booville kids went trick-or-treating together. Then, at eight o'clock, the group walked down the street, across a small field, and stopped at the bottom of Haunted Hill.

They looked up at the rickety, crickety house—with candles in the windows and smoke coming out of the chimneys.

The wind moaned.

The kids clung to each other.

"Come on, Wilson," Francine said at last. "Let's go solve this mystery."

The rest of the kids watched as Francine and Wilson made their way up the twisting rocky path on Haunted Hill.

There at the top was the old house. There was the cold, stone porch. There was the big wooden door. And there Francine and Wilson stopped—and stared.

"You knock!" Francine whispered to Wilson.

"I c-c-can't," Wilson whispered back. "My hands are busy clutching this sheet!"

Ah—oooo—oooo—ooooo! Screeeech! Bam-bam-a-lam-bam!
Clank—Clank—Ah—oooooo!

Weird, warbly, clanky noises were coming from inside the house!

"Let's go back!" cried Wilson.

"No way!" said Francine. "Let's look in the windows."

"But—but—"

It was no use. Wilson plodded along behind Francine as she tiptoed around the corner of the big house and crept up to a candlelit window. She inched up until she could peek over the windowsill.

"What do you see?" Wilson whispered.

"Boxes and crates—looks like somebody's moving in here. You should see this stuff!"

Wilson nervously tiptoed over and peeked in.
"Wow!"
"What are those things? Who would have weird stuff like that?"
asked Francine.
"I don't know," said Wilson. "Martians?"
Oooo—ooooo—ba—loo—loo!
"The sounds again!" said Francine. "They're coming from around
the next corner, I think."
Sssss—boom—bah—de—dah! Clank—Clank—Ah—oooooo!
"Yeah, well, I think *I've* seen enough! I'm getting outta—"
"Come on!"

Francine grabbed Wilson's sheet and sneaked along the house toward the next corner.

"Hey, I can't see!" cried Wilson.

"Shhh! I hear something! Wait. Something's around that corner!" whispered Francine.

"Oh—oh—I want to go home," moaned Wilson.

"Shhh! Let's just peek around. Slowly . . . slowly . . ."

"AGH!!!" screamed Wilson.

"AGH!!!" screamed Francine.

"AGH!!!" screamed Frank Junior, Denton, and Kate.

"What are you doing here?" said Francine, picking herself up off the ground.

"We were worried about you," said Denton. "We heard those noises—"

"So we came looking for you," added Kate.

"I still can't see!" cried Wilson.

"Come on! We gotta go look in that back window, Frankie!" said Francine.

"It's Frank *Junior*, if you please," mumbled her brother.

The Booville kids tiptoed quietly along the back of the house. Then, five wide-eyed faces peered into the back window.

"Cool! A drum set!" said Denton.

"Look at the keyboard!" said Kate.

"Very impressive sound amplification system," added Frank Junior.

"Wow! An electric guitar!" said Wilson.

"Look at those horns!" said Francine.

"Actually, we call those a trumpet and a tenor sax," said a strange voice.

The five wide-eyed faces turned around and stared into the darkness behind them.

"Who—who's talking?" asked Denton.

"Oh, hey! Sorry about that, cats! Here I am!"

The Booville kids watched as a white shape slowly appeared before them. It seemed to have a head—with big glowing eyes—and arms!

The white shape moved forward and stared at Wilson. Wilson stared back. The shape stared harder.

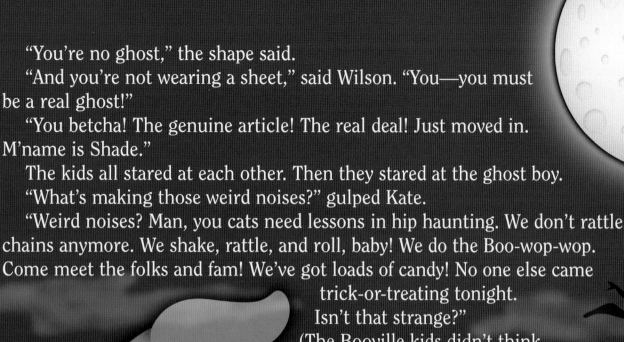

"You're no ghost," the shape said.

"And you're not wearing a sheet," said Wilson. "You—you must be a real ghost!"

"You betcha! The genuine article! The real deal! Just moved in. M'name is Shade."

The kids all stared at each other. Then they stared at the ghost boy.

"What's making those weird noises?" gulped Kate.

"Weird noises? Man, you cats need lessons in hip haunting. We don't rattle chains anymore. We shake, rattle, and roll, baby! We do the Boo-wop-wop. Come meet the folks and fam! We've got loads of candy! No one else came trick-or-treating tonight. Isn't that strange?" (The Booville kids didn't think that was strange.)

They all followed Shade—until he went right through the back door. They looked at each other—until the door creaked open.

"Come on in, cats. Step into my parlor. Mom? Dad? Sis? We've got our first trick-or-treaters!"

"Out-o-sight!" said the dad.

"Groovy!" said the mom.

"Boo-boo-be-doo!" squeaked his little sis.

"Let's crank up 'Do the Boogie Man Boogie'!" cried Shade.

The Booville kids couldn't believe their eyes—or ears—as the whole ghost family began whirling through the air, jazzing up the room.

Let's dance!" cried Francine, grabbing Wilson's hand.

Everyone danced and sang and howled and screamed 'til midnight. It was a blast! Frank Junior didn't even mind when Shade called him "Daddi-o."

It was the hippest Halloween ever—up there in the House on Haunted Hill!